Ambrose Lewis Vago

Phrenology vindicated: being a reply to the article by Dr Andrew Wilson, entitled "The old phrenology and the new", which appeared in "The gentleman's magazine", January, 1879

Antigonos

Ambrose Lewis Vago

Phrenology vindicated: being a reply to the article by Dr Andrew Wilson, entitled "The old phrenology and the new", which appeared in "The gentleman's magazine", January, 1879

Reprint of the original, first published in 1879.

1st Edition 2024 | ISBN: 978-3-38801-266-7

Antigonos Verlag is an imprint of Outlook Verlagsgesellschaft mbH.

Verlag (Publisher): Outlook Verlag GmbH, Zeilweg 44, 60439 Frankfurt, Deutschland, info@outlook-verlag.de
Vertretungsberechtigt (Authorized to represent): E. Roepke, Zeilweg 44, 60439 Frankfurt, Deutschland
Druck (Print): Libri Plureos GmbH, Friedensallee 273, 22763 Hamburg, Deutschland

PHRENOLOGY VINDICATED:

BEING

A REPLY TO THE ARTICLE BY
DR. ANDREW WILSON,

ENTITLED

"THE OLD PHRENOLOGY AND THE NEW,"

Which appeared in " The Gentleman's Magazine," January, 1879.

By A. L. VAGO.

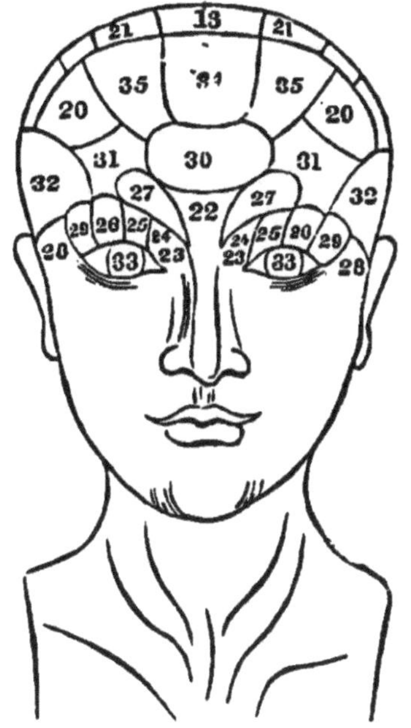

LONDON:

SIMPKIN, MARSHALL, & CO.

PHRENOLOGY VINDICATED.

To those who understand Phrenology and know something of its history, this will seem an unnecessary task, inasmuch as the objections of Doctor Andrew Wilson to Phrenology have often and long ago been raised, and which have already been shown to carry with them their own refutation.

It is not, however, with the view to reconquer that the present veto is assumed, but rather to rescue those who are apt to fall into the error of forming their judgments from an one-sided view of a subject which lays not an unimportant claim to our consideration.

The Doctor's article opens with the information that " There has ever lain a strange fascination for culture and ignorance alike, in the attempt to diagnose the intellect and character of man from the outward manifestations of his face and skull. The problem of character and its interpretation is as old as Plato, and may probably be shown to be more ancient still. Egyptian soothsayers and Babylonian astrologers were hardly likely ·to have omitted the indexing of character as a profitable and at the same time legitimate exercise of their art. The forecasting of future events and the casting of nativities were studies likely enough to bear a friendly relationship to the determination of character from the face, from fingers, or from skull and brain itself."

That in ages long past Egyptian soothsayers and Babylonian astrologers used to profess the forecasting of future events and the casting of nativities we have heard of before, and is no doubt quite true; but that with such sorcery they practised the art of reading character from the skull and brain itself is now intimated for the first time, and in terms so ambiguous as to expose the idea as both conjectural and presumptuous. With this kind of evidence it is now attempted to insinuate that Phrenology is all of a piece with the knavery practised by the impostors of old; unless it is intended to wrest the credit of the discovery of Phrenology from those to whom it is rightfully due.

The comment is scarcely deserved in this case, but it betokens a meagre intellect to ascribe to magic or witchcraft that which lies beyond our immediate comprehension. If the desire to know a man from his outward appearance were "as old as the hills," Phrenology is in no way traduced from being an outgrowth of such a desire. We do not ignore the science of astronomy from its discovery having succeeded a knack in our old grandmothers of watching the sky so as to judge of the weather.

Doctor Andrew Wilson says : " Nor shall we at present venture to oppose a scientific denial to Shakespeare's dictum that

' There is no art
To find the mind's construction in the face.' "

Unless the poet has been misquoted its denial must prove abortive. The face expresses nothing but the emotional feelings, and not anything of the sources from which such feelings spring. Conceal the head and we find in the face nothing expressive of any one of the intellectual powers. Persons trusting to physiognomic indications are apt to ascribe a certain amount of intelligence to a particular wink of the eye, which, to the adept, is known to be invariably employed to conceal ignorance ; while the really wise man mostly appears to be a greater fool than he is. The face therefore offers no clue to " the mind's construction."

Until the discovery of Phrenology there was no agreement arrived at as to the number and function of the primary or fundamental faculties of the mind. The speculations of the metaphysicians concerning the mind were so much in opposition one to the other that they have all been abandoned, and now the voluminous descantations of Locke, Stewart, Brown, Reid, and other writers of their school, have fallen into oblivion consequent on the introduction of Phrenology, which furnishes the only true philosophy of the mind.

While the metaphysicians were engaged in their elaborate propoundings of perception, conception, memory, abstraction, imagination, reason, and so forth, they never suspected that they were dealing but with terms that refer to qualities which merely characterise the various degrees and modes of operation of the faculties of the mind, and that such terms did not even serve to nominate or define the nature of a single elementary faculty of the mind. The discovery of this error was due to the doctrines of Phrenology; and now the phrenological nomenclature of the mental faculties has become general, while the terms perception, memory, and the like, have become obsolete as denominations of the special faculties of the mind.

Indeed the doctrines of Phrenology are now so generally accepted that their origin is altogether overlooked. Being unaware that the acknowledged philosophy of the mind is appreciable but in proportion as it is consistent with the principles of Phrenology, Dr. Andrew

Wilson says : " If the *old Phrenology*, or the science of brain-pans, be regarded as practically obsolete amongst physiologists and scientific men at large, what hopes of successfully estimating the ' coinage of the brain ' may the new Phrenology be said to hold out ? " Without anticipating the advantages of estimating the " coinage of the brain," as here promised to accrue from the *new Phrenology*, it would be interesting to know how long the old Phrenology has been regarded as obsolete among physiologists and scientific men. This idea must be of the Doctor's own coinage, and somewhat premature. Dr. Wilson has yet to learn that his masters, both as physiologists and scientific men, not only acknowledge the doctrines of Phrenology but advocate them in their writings. Among these are Mr. Abernethy, Mr. Lawrence, Dr. Samuel Solly, Dr. Mayo, Dr. Todd, Dr. Lardner, Dr. Laycock, Dr. Noble, Professor Hunter, M.D., and many others, whose works are still sought as standard guides to the medical student. These authorities are still held in the highest respect by the medical world, and each has given his unqualified support to Phrenology, and many of them regard with great honour its founders, Drs. Gall and Spurzheim.

We come now to that part of the Doctor's article where he asks : " How does the phrenological professor succeed very fairly in reading character?" which he answers thus: "His guide to character is in reality the face, not the brain-pan."

While Shakespeare, who must have been a keen observer of human nature, does not admit of finding the "mind's construction in the face," he speaks in the *Tempest* of "foreheads villainous low," and in *Hamlet* he attaches to the brow various powers, and says:

> "Where every god did seem to set his seal,
> To give the world assurance of a man."

As, notwithstanding this, many are inclined to regard the face as a better index of the mind than the head, we must refer the matter to a higher authority—no less than Lavater himself, who in his work "Physiognomy" says: "I pay more attention to the form and arching of the skull, as far as I am acquainted with it, than any of my predecessors," and that "I have considered this most firm, and least changeable, and far best defined part of the human body as the *foundation* of *physiognomy*."

Although the face may express a few fleeting emotions, such as mirth, rage, grief, surprise, horror, contempt, &c., it gives no information whatever of the general character, nor even of its component parts. In short, the face is but as the minute-hand of the mind's dial, the head the hour-hand, and the brain within its clock-works.

In another part we are informed by Dr. Wilson " That very few professors of Phrenology have ever studied the brain, whilst a large proportion may never have seen an actual human brain. Unless, therefore, one may logically maintain that total ignorance of the brain-pan is compatible with an accurate understanding of its contents and mysteries, the successful practice of Phrenology must be shown to depend on other data and other circumstances than are supplied by anatomy and physiology—these sciences admittedly supplying the foundation of all that is or can be known regarding the brain, its conformation, structure, and functions."

When persons seek the services of the phrenologist it is not to be instructed in the anatomy of the brain. Its structure and functions do not interest them. It is not of the internal structure of their heads that they wish to know, but of their mental qualifications; and for this purpose it is quite possible for one who is able to distinguish the various forms assumed by the head, and who understands the concomitant characteristics of each, to be able to estimate accurately the volume of the brain, and to interpret its features, without making a study of its mazy interior. Instances are not wanting where persons are able to tell a clock without understanding its works; nor are they the less capacitated for this from not having seen the works of a clock. To suppose otherwise would seem as preposterous as to consider it impossible to eat London sausages because we do not know what they are made of.

The successful practice of Phrenology does not, therefore, depend on a knowledge of either anatomy or physiology, and what may be more surprising is the fact that the discovery of Phrenology was not even due to these sciences; for previous to the dawn of Phrenology all they taught of the brain was how to slice it.

It was when a schoolboy that Gall observed the association of a particular mental power with a particular conformation of the head, remarking an absence of the latter where manifestations of the former did not present themselves. When at college, where he was educated for the medical profession, he continued his observations, noting a peculiar formation in the heads of such as were noted for any particular faculty; and when he found different persons with the same striking characteristics he also remarked a similarity in the form of their heads. In this manner he was led to surmise the connection of the mind with the head; but knowing that both the scalp and the skull took their conformation from that assumed by the brain, he made its anatomy his special study; and it is the care and labour which he, together with his coadjutor, Spurzheim, devoted to this subject that physiology and psychology have been rescued from comparative obscurity to their present high standing.

Dr. Wilson next informs us that "The fundamental doctrine of Phrenology is well-known to most of us. Its great doctrine is pictorially illustrated in the heads of the opticians' windows, and may be summed up in the statement that different parts or portions of the brain are the organs of different faculties of the mind. The brain thus viewed is a storehouse of faculties and qualities, each faculty possessing a dominion and sphere of its own amongst the cerebral substance. Thus, if Phrenology be credited with materialising mind in the grossest possible fashion, its votaries have themselves and their science to thank for this aspersion." How the mind becomes materialised by its connection with the brain the Doctor does not explain; he merely assumes that it is. In viewing the brain as a " store-house of faculties and qualities " he has stumbled upon an error of his own making, which forms no part of the doctrines of Phrenology. Here he confounds organ with function, a fault altogether unpardonable in a physiologist. He seems to forget—if ever he learned it—that faculty, or function, is a quality belonging to an organ, and is not the organ itself. It is conceivable to the meanest capacity, that electricity is a power distinct from the battery through which its operations are conducted. No one of sound mind would confound the one with the other on account of their connection.

Dr. Wilson continues: "If it be maintained that feelings of *Destructiveness* reside above the ear then must we localise the desire to kill or destroy in so much brain substance as lies included in the 'bump.'" Thus couched, the idea may seem very funny, perhaps ridiculous, but to know that such a feeling as destructiveness forms an element of the human mind, we have but to reflect on the work that has lately been going on between the Russians and the Turks, and that now going on between the English and the Zulus. Even in individuals, where is the sportsman that does not delight more in killing than in eating what he bags? Ladies will sometimes chase a tiny insect to death to secure repose at night, and in some instances, just for the pleasure it affords. But as a faculty of the mind it must not be adjudged by its abuses. Our protection and preservation make it essential, and being *innate* it cannot be but of "origin divine," however much, by an affectatious sentimentality, we may be opposed to its presence in the list of the mind's faculties. While the word destructiveness serves as the best term afforded by the English language to designate and define the nature of the faculty so named, it is to be regretted that it should, at the same time, convey the idea of its abuse rather than that of its use. But if this, or any other power of the mind, performs its functions through a particular part of the brain, the student in this branch of enquiry will not on this account feel himself degraded more than the physiologist, whose science teaches him to regard the eye as the organ of sight, or who may, with impunity, lay his finger on his nose and tell us it is the organ of smell. But what of its dignity would the mind lose if it were material that so much dread is entertained about the idea? Certainly nothing on account of any light that would be thrown on the subject; for the mind's subtilty is not a whit more inexplicable than matter, however gross. To all capable of contemplation, matter presents itself as both marvellous and incomprehensible. Its annihilation is impossible, for we cannot take from nor add to a single particle of the material world. More cannot be said of the mind. How, then, is it aspersed by its association with the brain?

To look at the marked heads through an optician's window is a poor—not to say a mean—way of seeking information concerning the doctrines of Phrenology: as well might we look on a map of England to discover its history.

Doctor Wilson says: "When vain-glory besets us we must hold, if we are phrenologists, that there is a molecular stirage and activity of brain particles beneath a certain bump of '*self-esteem*' situated above and in front of the ear." Assuming that we are phrenologists we should, for that reason, hold nothing of the kind, for then we should know that vain-glory is a derivation not of self-esteem but of love of approbation, and that the organ of self-esteem is not situated above and in front of the ear, but up at the back part of the head.

We come now to consider what Doctor Wilson is pleased to call a "molecular stirage of brain particles." There is throughout the entire surface of the brain a constant palpitation, and this process is essential to the growth and healthful condition of the brain. That a given part of the brain becomes more than usually active during the exercise of a given faculty is an ascertained fact, and as such the phrenologist is quite willing to recognise it, and to abide the consequences.

Even though the mind's connection with the brain be viewed as merely hypothetical, no physiologist, having regard for his reputation, will venture to assert that the brain's action is not impelled or increased by mental excitement, be what may its kind.

Doctor Andrew Wilson next tells us: "Were the deductions of Phrenology true, or were its claims to be regarded as a science founded on definite grounds, mind could no longer be regarded as a mystery, since it would be within the power of the phrenologist to assert that when swayed by emotions of one kind or another he could declare which part of the brain was being affected. This declaration logically follows upon that which maintains the localisation ˙of faculties in different parts of the brain ; but it is a conclusion at the same time from which physiology simply retires in outspoken disdain as presenting us with an empirical explanation of mysteries to which the furthest science has yet failed to attain."

Now what should one know about the deductions of Phrenology who has never learned so much as the situations of the organs, and who is incapable of discriminating their functional differences ? We shall see. " Were the deductions of Phrenology true mind could no longer be regarded as a mystery." That anything so fulsome should come from the pen of one holding the honourable degree of doctor, and that it should be forced upon the notice of a respectable public, is a mystery outdoing even itself.

If it were not that we have it in " black and white " it would be scarcely possible to credit that anyone could be found so mentally feeble as to desire the mind to remain a mystery. Were we to be attacked by an epidemic which should puzzle the physician to treat or allay we should regard our condition as lamentable in the extreme.   As most of us would rather suffer ill-health than unsoundness of mind, it has, for this reason, been the first and highest aim of the philosopher to dispel the mystery in which the mind has been so long involved, and this, that we should the better understand the care and treatment of the mind, the healthful condition of which we should prize more than life itself.

It is due to phrenological teaching that we now know that the mind, owing to its relationship with the body, is, like its tenement, governed by laws.

"The old metaphysical idea that the mind is free, unbounded, unfettered, illimitable, and all the rest of it, may appear very well in romance, which is its only legitimate province, but in the philosophy of mind it should have no place.   It may please the ear, but it has only fine words, and not truth, for its foundation.   The mind may be unbounded by being able in its imaginings to rove unrestrainedly to any point in space—to soar above to the highest heavens, or to dive down into the lowest pit of Erebus; but sometimes the mind, in its wanderings, goes too far to get back again, and where, then, is its boundless freedom?   Until we rid ourselves of this sublime delusion about the mind's freedom, and learn to know that, subtle as it is, the mind is subject to certain laws, there can be no such thing as a judicious management of the mind, and both folly and madness will, as hitherto, remain insolvable mysteries. But when we learn that the mind, like the body, is strengthened and improved by exercise; that its perfect development depends upon a variety of exercises; that it becomes distorted if its parts are unequally exercised; that it dwindles and degenerates from inactivity, is liable to disease, is disabled if over-wrought; or that it is either excited or depressed by intemperance; when we learn that disease of mind is thus effected, and, like disease of the body, is transmitted from parents to children, and that we cannot long continue to indulge the passions or propensities to the neglect of our moral and intellectual nature without enfeebling and deranging the mind, and without the risk of having to rear a family of idiots, we may then discover the true source of folly and madness, and know better how to avoid the ways that lead to them. When we begin to attend to these facts, and dismiss the old high-sounding and fallacious theories about the mind, and become observant of the laws by which the mind is governed, we may hope to secure for our trouble that genial harmony between the faculties upon which depends the happiness of the mind, and without which life itself becomes un-desirable and its pleasures joyless."*

* Transcribed from "Orthodox Phrenology," 2nd edition. 2s. London: Simpkin & Marshall.

B

While Phrenology thus informs us of the nature of the mind, it affords no explanation of its mystery. But Dr. Wilson is under the impression that much less than this will serve to remove the mystery by which the mind is surrounded. He thinks, presuming Phrenology to be true, that the phrenologist has only to point out which part of the brain is being affected when the mind is swayed by one or other emotion, and the thing is done. And then he tells us: " This declaration *logically* follows upon that which maintains the localisation of faculties in different parts of the brain." Did ever mountebank utter such charlatanry? That the corporeal organs occupy different parts of the body is a physiological fact; and perfectly consistent with this is the phrenological proposition that the organs of the mental faculties occupy different parts of the brain; yet this, Dr. Wilson says, " is a conclusion from which physiology simply retires in outspoken disdain." Here the Doctor should speak for himself, and not in the name of physiology seek shelter for blurting such nonsense. Until the recognition of Phrenology there was no physiology of the brain; even its anatomy was imperfectly known. It was the phrenologist, Dr. Spurzheim, who, with a brain in one hand and a spatula in the other, proved, what was not known to the medical world before, that the brain in most part consisted of fibrous matter, and that these fibres or nerves served, one set to convey sensation, the other to conduct motive-power. The cerebral anatomy of the phrenologists, Drs. Gall and Spurzheim, has been appropriated in physiological works without any open acknowledgment, except in a few honourable instances. On this account the newly-fledged physiologist is not aware how much his science is indebted to Phrenology; and so, in his ignorance, he feels himself justified in coming forward to splutter his views against Phrenology, skimmed from no better source than that supplied by its itinerant professors, and a peep at the phrenological heads in an optician's window.

While the physiology of Phrenology has been begged, borrowed, and stolen by the medical world on the one hand, and its philosophy unacknowledgedly assumed by the scientific world on the other, it is now recognised only in its denuded state. Divested of all but its phraseology, it is spurned with contumely, and disowned by all but the professor whose living depends upon its practice, and in whose hands it has every chance of being basely murdered. Notwithstanding this, its epitaph is not yet needed, for Phrenology still lives, if but in the works of its despoilers.

The beneficial influence of its doctrines has been recognised by physicians in cases of mental aberration;

and now, in place of the old strait-jacket remedy, which but aggravated the condition of the patient, the milder treatment of its suggestion has been adopted, with infinitely better results. In fact, phrenological principles, forming, as they now do, an under-current in so many departments of science, their source has become so intricate as to be lost sight of altogether.

Dr. Wilson says : "That we may duly understand not merely the falsity of the old Phrenology but the bearings of the new aspects of brain-science, as revealed by modern physiology, we must briefly glance at the general conformation of the brain." Does he suppose that J. Spurzheim, M.D., the propounder of Phrenology, holding degrees of the Universities of Vienna and Paris, and being, as he was, a licentiate of the Royal College of Physicians of London, could have known less about the conformation of the brain than we shall glean from a brief glance at it ; that we should understand the falsity of Phrenology, in which particular he altogether failed ?

Brief glances tend only to the common error of imposing upon ourselves false notions, which we sometimes rashly proffer to refute what we do not understand. Ignorance is infinitely preferable to error, for ignorance is open to truth, while error but usurps its place and leaves truth an outcast.

In giving his brief glance at the conformation of the brain Dr. Wilson says : " The organ of mind, contained within the skull, consists of the greater brain, or cerebrum, and the lesser brain, or cerebellum."

Why, what language is this? What can he mean by " the organ of mind contained within the skull?" Is he going to lump the mind into a single unit and claim two brains for its organ ? If this is a specimen of the new Phrenology, what next may we expect? It certainly has one advantage over the old, for instead of being at the trouble of pointing to particular parts of the head to explain away the mystery of the mind, now, according to his own logic, the Doctor has only to lay his hand on his head, the mystery flies, and lo! all is quite plain and simple.

In the course of his brief glance at the conformation of the brain Dr. Wilson informs us that " the brain substance consists of white and grey nervous matter. The grey matter forms the outermost layer, and encloses the white; in the grey matter thought is chiefly evolved, and the white matter merely conveys nervous impressions." While Dr. Wilson preaches up this as the physiology of the brain it is a pity he does not know something of Phrenology, so that he might recognise it when he sees it, and save exposing himself in the ridiculous position of presenting a common fact as a newly discovered wonder. If this is to form the basis of the new Phrenology, we cannot regard its foundation but as both second-hand and stolen. It is possible that objects may be found on ground where they had been previously overlooked, and, if only sprats come to our nets, let us not deny there are finer fish in the sea. In the case of modern physiologists, not anything in the cerebral, or nervous system, has been discovered which had not been previously considered and explained by the phrenologists, other than positive proof of the truth of the doctrines which these advanced—namely, that different parts of the brain perform different and distinct functions, and, therefore, the brain is not a single organ, but a congeries of several organs.

In another part of his article Dr. Wilson says: "The phrenological doctrine of the disposition of faculties must be held to include the idea that, the larger the brain, the better specialised should be the mental faculties of the individual; the greater the amount of brain-substance, forming the good and bad qualities and regions of the phrenologists, the more active should be the mental organisation. Now, it is a patent fact that this rule tells strongly against the phrenologist's assumption. True, various great men have had large brains; but cases of great men possessing small brains are equally common, as also are instances where insanity and idiocy were associated with brains of large size."

Phrenologists have not left it to be merely surmised, but have given it as one of the propositions of Phrenology, that the cerebral organs are developed each in proportion to the power of its particular function. Of course this applies to the whole of the brain, although not always when individual is compared with individual, because these often differ in temperament or constitutional condition. This, though often overlooked by " outsiders," is never lost sight of by the phrenologist, who well knows that the brain, from being all of a piece with the rest of the body, partakes of its general qualities. If, therefore, he sees a man all blubber and puff, he attaches no importance to his head, although it were as large as the dome of St. Paul's. Not so when the temperament is refined, which is known by a compactness of texture, seen in the face, and shown by the general proportions of the body. When, in reference to the mental faculties, Dr. Wilson speaks of "good and bad qualities," he makes use of language which shows that he does not understand Phrenology, for there are no bad faculties—it is only their abuse that is regarded as bad.

Cases of great men having small heads being common is not at all surprising to the phrenologist.

Many men regarded as great are not generally so, but great only in a particular department; and as but few of the mental faculties serve in such cases, the entire bulk of brain may be comparatively small.

Where the head is large in cases of idiocy or insanity, the brain is either diseased or deranged in its structure; and then its size and form go for nothing.

What may seem more puzzling than any of the instances quoted by Dr. Wilson is the fact observed by phrenologists, that men of common every-day life are often met with having heads in configuration and density equal to those of the greatest men that ever lived. This, if anything, should settle the question against the phrenologist; and yet not altogether so: it is not what is publicly known of a man that should decide the extent of his thoughts and feelings, for often the man who thinks and feels most expresses the least.

We need not follow the Doctor in his learned disquisition of the brain in its fœtal state; for the naturalist learns nothing concerning the branches, leaves, flowers, and fruits of a plant from inspecting its seed.

Dr. Wilson very justly observes: "The *scalpel* of the anatomist can nowhere discover in the full-grown brain an organ of Veneration, or of Hope, or of Language, or of Destructiveness, or of any other mental feature; nor can his *microscope* detect in Nature's wondrous process of fashioning the brain any reason for the belief that the organ of mind is a collection of parts, each devoted to the exercise of a special quality of mind."

The phrenologist is quite willing to admit all this, and more; not only that the scalpel and the microscope are of no use in the matter, but also the anatomist's own eyes; for, without previously knowing it, he might look at a severed tongue till he goes blind without being able to discern its function. There is nothing in the formation of the tongue to show that it is susceptible of impressions from flavours; or that it talked English, or talked Irish, or talked French, or talked Dutch. Though he may be aided by every instrument in his cabinet the anatomist will find nothing in the appearance of either the optic, auditory, olfactory or gloso-pharyngeal nerves to bespeak their respective function. In fact, anatomy vouchsafes nothing respecting the function of any organ in the animal system. Upon anatomical evidence *alone* it is not only unjustifiable but presumptuous in the extreme even to regard the brain as the organ of the mind.

The anatomist may cut into the brain, scrape it, wash it, turn it inside out or upside down; then he may know something of its structure, but anything beyond this is quite beside his art. When the physiologist steps in, it is quite another affair. He learns from the anatomist that below the surface of the brain are thousands of fibres, which singly are of impalpable fineness ; that these, from their termini within the lobules of the two sides, or cerebral hemispheres, take an inward course, and run together in lines towards the centre, where they severally intercross and pass downward together, forming a narrow column purposely to thread the aperture at the base of the skull, and continue in their channel along the vertebræ, from which they branch out to every part of the body. After this is discovered by the anatomist it falls to the province of the physiologist to ascertain the use and end of it all.

The fibres of the brain perform each a special duty. They are not few—the anatomist does not yet know their number—and every one is an organ subserving to a particular function, which no other can undertake. As Shakespeare says : "The *eye* of man hath not *heard*, the *ear* of man hath not *seen*, man's hand is not able to taste."

Then there is the mechanism of the brain to be explained. The brain in its entirety presents itself as an extremely delicate and complicated piece of machinery. All its fibres are connected only by the surface or grey matter of the brain.

Notwithstanding the infinite adjustment of parts in the ear and eye, the impressions made upon them from without are not recognised if their respective nerves are intercepted at any part before reaching the interior surface of the brain. These matters are for the physiologist to explain, who, when he makes the brain and its functions his especial study, must arrive at the conclusion that Phrenology furnishes the only physiology consistent with the anatomy of the brain. To accomplish this the student should not shut himself entirely in the dissecting-room; but he must also engage in the study of mental phenomena, where, as he becomes experienced in this department, he will recognise the phrenological analysis of the human mind as the best system of mental science that has hitherto been presented to the world.

Dr. Wilson states: "There is not a trace of a single organ such as the phrenologist theoretically maintains is represented in the brain." This is contradicted by the drawings of the brain given with the Doctor's article. Then he adds: "There is no division into separate parts and portions, as the phrenologist's charts would lead the observer to suppose. The arrangement which appears so clear on the phrenologist's bust is nowhere represented in the brain itself."

The phrenological busts are intended to give the student a knowledge of the whereabouts or situations of the organs, and not at all to lead the observer to suppose that the brain is done up into separate parcels, and labelled according to the nature of their contents, as Dr. Wilson seems to imply that it should be, or that Phrenology cannot be true.

In stating that there is no division in the brain corresponding to the phrenological organs the Doctor

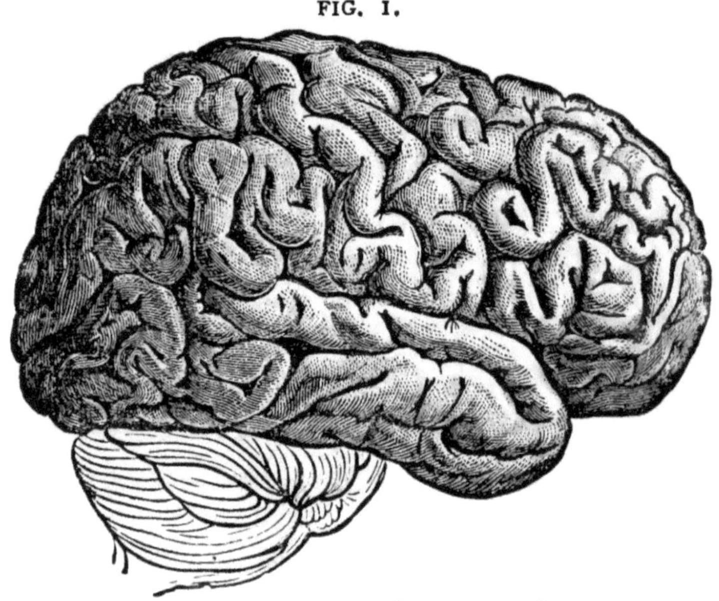

FIG. I.

HUMAN BRAIN. (SIDE VIEW.)

exposes himself as being ignorant of the anatomy of the brain; for Dr. Spurzheim, in reference to a natural division between the convolutions, says : "Vertical slices of the convolutions, macerated in nitric acid diluted with rectified alcohol, or in pure alcohol, become hard, and are most easily divided in the middle line. The separation into two layers is also exhibited when the convolutions are boiled for twelve or fifteen minutes in oil. When through a tube we blow on such a slice, or when with a syringe we direct against it a small stream of water, the separation may be made in the middle very easily; but at the sides not at all without obviously destroying the structure of the fibres. In the two latter cases especially, the two surfaces which are separated remain smooth ; nor is there any division of vessels, or any traces of fibres passing from one side to the other. The existence of the two layers of the convolutions must consequently be admitted. Nevertheless it may be that between them there exists an adhesion of contiguity, maintained, perhaps, by a fine cellular membrane ; but there is by no means a connection of contiguity produced by an intermixture and confusion of substance. The junction of the two layers may be denominated agglutination, but not concretion."

Here we find that by a very delicate process of investigation it is ascertained that the brain is in its structure composed of various parts ; and that what Dr. Wilson says is but "theoretically maintained" is nothing less than an indubitable fact.

If the organs of the brain stood isolated, as Dr. Wilson thinks it is necessary that they should to prove their existence, the brain, as an instrument of the mind, could not so well answer its uses as if its surface were all one piece, and without divisions. It is by the immediate contiguity of the cerebral organs, one to another, that a line of communication is maintained between them, consistent with that power among the faculties of acting consecutively and in concert, and without which power our ideas would be incoherent and disconnected. Hence, in cases of concussion of the brain, where this order is disturbed, the mind is often found to wander.

The constitution of the mind in its normal state would not, therefore, admit of such sections in the brain as Dr. Wilson would desire, as co-operation between the functions of its organs would then be impossible.

It is by the entirety of the brain that its different functions possess the power of acting collectively.

When an appeal is made to a man's *Benevolence* for some charitable object, before he puts his hand into his pocket, his *calculating power* is brought into action and consults with his *Acquisitiveness* as to how much he should give ; and then he acts in accordance with the decision arrived at after such consultation between the faculties interested has been held. Now these faculties being able thus to commune one with another for a given purpose, and each having an organ in the brain, it is necessary that the cerebral organs should be connected just as we find them in the brain's surface. The fibres, underlying the surface of the brain, as previously described, serve, like telegraphic wires, to convey messages from the brain through the spinal cord and direct the movements of the body, so as in action to accomplish the will or end desired.

Although the folds or convolutions of the brain serve as boundary marks for the phrenological organs, it is well known that their object is to give to the brain a greater amount of surface, necessary for its operations, than it could have within the space of the skull, if it were even and not corrugated; just as space is economised in the electric battery by its necessary great length of wire being coiled up.

But the phrenologist seeks not for organs in bundles. He knows well enough that Nature, in her handiwork, conceals a variety of organs within a smooth surface, and in such manner as to defy their detection.

In the worm that crawls it is impossible to see, even in a rudimentary form, the wings with which it ultimately flies. The newly-laid egg shows no separate parts to represent the organs which jointly constitute the chicken. Notwithstanding this we do not doubt, we do not merely believe, but we know from experience, that in this apparent uniform substance is contained the principles of a beak, eyes, tongue, lungs, gizzard, heart, legs, wings, and of thousands of other organs.

The epidermis, which covers the body of the chicken,

is all one piece, and yet it contains organs so numerous that to count them would be no easy task. Each of these organs is distinct, and performs the office of supplying a feather of a particular shape, size, and colour to suit the part it covers, and on which depends that

FIG. 2.

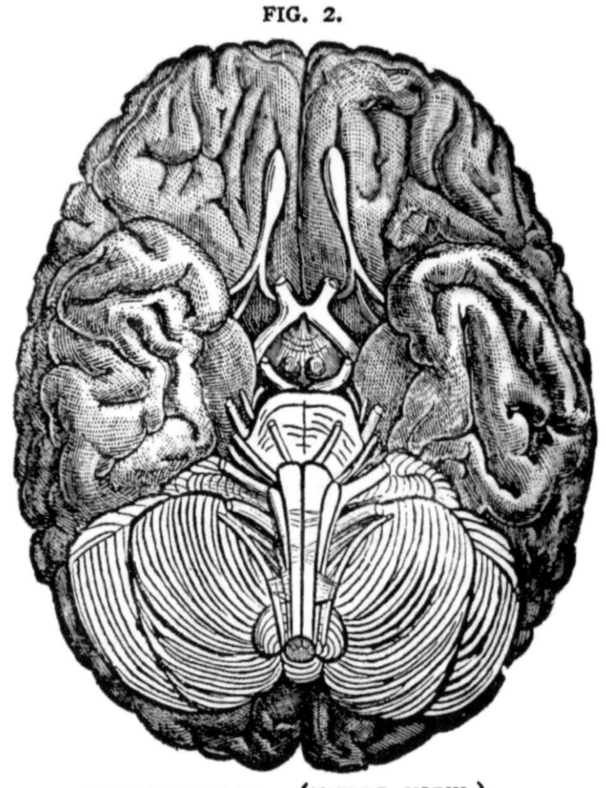

HUMAN BRAIN.　(UNDER VIEW.)

symmetry of form and diversity of scintilating shades seen in the plumage of the fully-fledged bird ; so gorgeous in the peacock, and not absent in the little sparrow.

Dr. Wilson says: "Moreover, one very important consideration will dawn upon the reflective mind which considers that the convolutions of the brain are not limited to the crown and sides of the head, but, on the contrary, extend over the entire surface of the cerebrum, and are developed on its base (see fig. 2). No phrenologist has attempted, it is true, to get at the base of the brain by inspecting the palate ; but it would be regarded as an absurd and unwarrantable statement to assert that the base of the brain has no functions, and that the mind of man is located only at the top and sides of the head. Yet the phrenologist is in the position of one making such an assertion, since his science takes no account of the base or internal parts of the brain—situations, forsooth, in which anatomy and the newer Phrenology demonstrate the existence of very important sensory and other organs."

All this would, of course, naturally suggest itself to one whose knowledge of Phrenology and what it teaches of the offices of the brain had been derived from a brief glance at a phrenological head in an optician's window. Anatomy certainly does point to convolutions at the base of the brain that are not represented in the phrenological bust, but not to the number that Dr. Wilson would imply by refering us to the diagram of " base of brain." In all drawings of convex objects, a very great deal is included that belongs to the sides, which is particularly conspicuous in this instance. All the convolutions shown in the diagram, at the front part of the brain, consist of the organs indicated in the phrenological geography of the head, and named according to their respective functions, Individuality, Form, Size, Weight, Colour, Order and Number; while the convolutions at the other sides represent organs marked in the phrenological head that reach up to the second tier.   In this manner nearly one-half of the brain is drawn into the diagram, which, without scruple, is presented to us as representing only the base. The organs marked on the lower sides of the head do not terminate abruptly as in the bust, but continue under, and thus comprise many of the convolutions at the base of the brain.   When we consider this, and deduct from the diagram the convolutions belonging to the sides of the brain, we shall find left at the base not more than four or five that are not accounted for in the bust.   These convolutions, omitted in the bust, will be seen in the diagram (fig. 2) to constitute the termini, or gangliæ, of the optic, auditory, and other nerves which communicate with the external world.

But phrenologists never supposed that their list included all the mental faculties, nor yet all the cerebral organs.

To assume from the silence of phrenologists concerning the innermost parts of the brain that they thereby hold the position of asserting that such parts are functionless—and to vilify them for it into the bargain—is but even with the moral mistake of misrepresenting the number of the convolutions at the base of the brain, and may redound to the credit of at least one champion of the new Phrenology.

It will be remembered that Dr. Wilson has already told us that there is no trace of a single organ in the brain to justify the phrenological theory which claims the brain as a congeries of organs; and now he tells us of "situations, forsooth (in the brain), in which anatomy and the newer Phrenology demonstrate the existence of very important sensory and other organs."

This looks queer; it does not promise much for modern physiology when it leads to conclusions so diverse respecting the brain. First she would, and then she wouldn't. A creature so fickle need not have been so proud as to "retire in outspoken disdain" to hide its own paternity.

Dr. Wilson, as he proceeds, says: "The form of the skull is dependent on the amount and disposition of the white matter, and not on that of the grey; and the former, as we have seen, has but a minor influence or part in the mental constitution, since its function is merely that of conducting, and not originating, thoughts and impressions. Since, then, Phrenology lays so much stress on skull conformation as a clue to brain structure, it must be regarded as dealing rather with the results of the disposition of the white matter than with that of the grey, and this latter assumption of necessity involves a second—namely, that Phrenology has no status as a science of mind at all."

Here he plainly tells us that the function of the white matter is that of conducting thoughts and impressions. In the brief glance which he gives of the conformation of the brain, he says: "That it is in the grey matter that thought is chiefly evolved." Be it remembered that hitherto Dr. Wilson has furnished no explanation for assuming these positions, and by ignoring Phrenology he has no right to assume them; for, if the connection between the mind and brain has a scientific basis at all, it is alone due to Phrenology; therefore, excepting the claims of Phrenology, we have them only upon his bare word: however, we will take them for granted.

In the grey matter thought is evolved; the white conducts thought. If no thought is evolved in the grey matter there will be none for the white to conduct. Nothing going on at headquarters, the messengers have nothing to do—both resting idle—result: both dwindle, soften, too poor to keep up appearances; outside show, mean. On the other hand, much thought evolved in the grey matter, its correspondence with the outer world is necessarily increased, its messengers (the white matter) have much to carry, and both being engaged, though differently yet together, in the same office, they, by exercise, develop together and become strengthened to the extent of being able to enlarge their premises—result: a larger edifice seen from without. Thus, the grey and the white matter, though differently employed, are employed in the same office and conduce to the same end. The grey represents the master, the white his servants, and by their livery (outside show in the skull) we judge of the wealth or power of the master ; and by the kind of errands (mental characteristics, either enacted or expressed) performed by these servants we judge of the business of the master. Thus, with his own premises, is explained another of the contorted riddles of Dr. Wilson ; and, if " Phrenology has no status as a science of mind at all," it is, nevertheless, the physiology of the brain.

But the idea that thought is evolved in the grey matter is a step in advance of the *old Phrenology;* it must therefore be a discovery of the *new Phrenology ;* and by all that is fair and honourable let it keep its own. Phrenologists never went so far as to assert that thought is evolved in any part of the brain. They regard the brain as conducive to mental manifestations ; as the instrument through which the mind holds communication with the world exterior to itself; like the telescope through which is seen the ship at sea, which is neither the ship nor the sight, although the ship may be lost to sight without it.

The white matter consists of several bundles of fibres which emerge from the centre and radiate to the surface, where they meet the grey matter which covers them. Besides serving the purpose of thus holding the cerebral organs together, and so prevent derangement from the violence of coughing, sneezing, and such convulsions, the grey matter has a function altogether different to that assumed of it by Dr. Wilson, when he informs us that in it "*thought is evolved.*" Indeed, if so little is known of the grey matter that the modern physiologist is allowed to proclaim such as its function, even without support from any data, the science of cerebral physiology can be making but a retrograde movement since the days of Drs. Gall and Spurzheim.

While the actual function of the grey matter of the brain has for years been presenting itself in full glare before our notice, the modern physiologist has utterly failed to detect it; dangling, as it were, so closely within reach of the new-fangled Phrenology of Dr. Wilson, and yet to be missed—worse than all a falsity grasped—and this part of the brain's fabric misapplied.

It is from not knowing the function of the grey substance in the brain that physiologists, in their investigations of the brain in its diseased states, have been led to form such erratic conclusions regarding the claims of Phrenology. Whilst such knowledge would dispel all contentious bickering among physiologists on this subject, it would, at the same time, suggest a method of treatment, with probability of success, in cases that still continue to be neglected as hopeless.

To state here what is the function of the grey matter of the brain without first considering the evidences which point to it as such, would be premature; and coming from one outside or not of the medical faculty, it would be presumptuous in the extreme; but when the necessary evidence is adduced, as it will appear in further considering the article of Dr. Wilson, then its disclosure may be laughed at, the fact denied, shown to be false because it was not discovered before, absurd for not being revealed by an M.D., F.R.C.S., and all the rest of it, and it may be proved to be totally impossible that a discovery so simple should un-mystify the medical world in a matter that has puzzled it from all eternity.

To the phrenological organs of the perceptive faculties, namely, Individuality, Form, Size, Colour, Order, and Number, which are mapped along the brow of the eye, Dr. Wilson objects: "How may we know when one encroaches upon another to the exclusion, or atrophy, of the latter?"

Does he suppose that the skull, like a tight-fitting boot which jumbles the toes out of their natural position and cripples the foot, was designed by a bungler, and in such manner as to frustrate the end which it serves, namely, to shield and protect the brain; and by such trash, uttered in the name of anatomy, to quash the claims of Phrenology? This is another specimen of his *brief glance*, and such as every anatomist would repudiate.

The next charge brought against Phrenology by Dr. Wilson is worth considering on account of its laughableness. In the usual loudness of his great learning in anatomy, he says : "But the anatomist has also something of importance to say regarding the actual existence of certain of the organs of mind mapped out by the phrenologist. Leaning trustfully upon their emperical deductions, the phrenologists have frequently localised faculties and organs of mind upon bony surfaces separated from the brain by an intervening space of considerable kind. In so far as comparative anatomy is concerned, Phrenology receives no assistance in its attempt to localise mind-functions in man. An elephant is admittedly a sagacious animal, with a brain worth studying; just as a cat or tiger presents us with a disposition in which—if brain-science is applicable, as it should be, to lower forms of life exhibiting special traits of character—Destructiveness should be well represented and typically illustrated. Alas for Phrenology! the bump of Destructiveness in the feline races resolves itself into a mass of jaw-muscles, and the elephant's brain is placed certainly not within a foot or so of the most skilful of phrenological digits. The 'frontal sinuses,' or great air-spaces in the forehead bones of the animal, intervene between the front of the brain— the region, *par excellence*, of intellect, according to Phrenology—and the outside layer of the skull; so that an observer could no more accurately construct a phrenological chart of an elephant than he could diagnose the contents of a warehouse by scanning the exterior of the building."

Alas for Phrenology, indeed, when we find anyone seeking the organ of Destructiveness in jaw-muscles! and all hail the new Phrenology, which in jaw-muscles seeks the destruction of the old! When he tells us that the brain of the elephant lies a foot or so behind the *oss frontis*, perhaps he knows all about it, and, for his purpose, he might just as well tell us that the elephant's brain lay ten thousand miles away. It will be time enough to set up the elephant as a standard to test the truth of Phrenology when it is proved that what it teaches about the human brain was discovered under a bushel. And what does it prove against Phrenology if "an observer cannot accurately construct a phreno-logical chart of an elephant?" Are we to decry the microscope because it does not enable us to see in the dark?

With this as a prelude comes "the old, old story" of the frontal sinus, which, he says, "man as well as the elephant possesses." Yes, but what an odious com-parison! and this he calls comparative anatomy, from which, he says, Phrenology receives no assistance. But Phrenology does not need its assistance. Comparative anatomy is not to be relied on as deciding the position and function of the organs of the body; for while one class of animals shows the muscles of the body to lie out-side the bones, the lobster class shows them to lie within. While mastication in most animals is performed by the teeth in the mouth, this process in birds—which, as we know, have no teeth—is performed by the gizzard, which is within the body, and right away from the mouth. So much, then, for his comparative anatomy.

The frontal sinus of the human head, he says, is "of considerable extent, in some cases exceeding an inch." A frontal sinus such as this we may sometimes read about, but very seldom see ; and, excepting in very old age, would be accounted as a monstrosity. This cavity in the frontal bone generally begins at the age of twelve years, and gradually increases with age, but barely ever reaches beyond a half-inch from front to back. The frontal sinus is always allowed for by the phrenologist, who, being acquainted with the characteristics accompanying each different type of head, may give very accurate estimates even without considering what

FIG. 3.

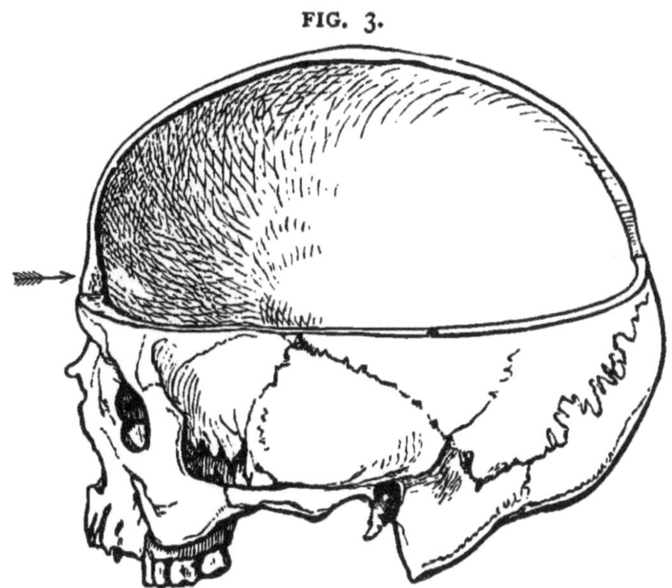

HUMAN SKULL SHOWING FRONTAL SINUS.   DRAWN FROM NATURE.

is thus supposed to lie in his way—just as the sculptor who, never having heard of gravitation, yet observes its laws in every stroke he makes against the marble.

Dr. Wilson relates of a Mr. Stone, who, when President of the Royal Medical Society of Edinburgh in 1829, read a paper referring to measurements made by him from one hundred human skulls of well-known persons ;

and by these measurements Mr. Stone demonstrated that the skulls of fifteen murderers, whose crimes had been marked by unusual brutality and violence, were superior in phrenological configuration to the skull of Dr. David Gregory, once Professor of Mathematics in the University of Edinburgh, and Savilian Professor of Astronomy at Oxford, a friend and contemporary of Sir Isaac Newton, and whose character was well known as that of an amiable, accomplished, intellectual man.

In his self-imposed delusion that fitful actions should be accounted for by cerebral proclivities, Mr. Stone, and now Dr. Wilson, sought a capital set-off against Phrenology in the laborious, conscientious, and no doubt unbiased observations contained in that wonderful paper.

The word murderer very justly bears a most frightful signification, yet murderers, apart from the circumstances which bring upon them this appellation, have been known to be humane, amiable, accomplished, and intellectual. We have had them crop up from among the clergy, the medical world, and other bodies, involving the highest intellectual accomplishments, even the passion-restraining Quakers included.

Men of high moral character, holding most honourable positions, by frequent interruptions while conducting their arduous duties, are subject to vexations often exceeding in intensity what, under some circumstances, would goad to desperation. This state of feeling will sometimes find vent in a silent imprecation, while the dignity of office demands it to be cloaked by courtesy or an affected affability. Disengaged from the aggravating turmoils of office, each man as he joins his family is seized on all sides by his children, and lovingly hugged as the dearest and kindest dad in all the world, although each one knows that he is most fearful in wrath. This is human nature un-Chesterfield-ised ; just as we find it in the knight and the squire, in the king and his most humble subject. But where do we find a system so appositely explaining these apparently opposite qualities in each individual of the human race as Phrenology, by representing the mind as consisting of animal propensities, moral sentiments, and intellectual faculties? And what deplorable ignorance to regard as *bad* those *propensities* so essential to support the animal frame of man, on the healthful condition of which depends the power of conducting his intellectual and moral duties.

Be the propensities good or bad, we all feel at times an internal conflict between duty and passion. Indeed, it is to remind and guard us against the evil consequences of yielding the wrong way that we feel the necessity of retaining my Lord Bishop and his enormous staff; life consisting, as it does from beginning to end, of a continuous sinning and repenting. Phrenology, then, is not proved to be false because our heads are not better formed than those of others who have unguardedly enacted the evils to which, in thought, we are all prone. Phrenology cannot be justly implicated as false even though we do find those who have once or twice exceeded the law, having heads similar to those of others who have all along been standing on the very brink of that dangerous point.

Phrenology treats of thoughts and feelings, and not of rare and occasional spasmodic actions. Each faculty of the mind may be exercised in many different ways. The particular kind of exercise from which an organ becomes developed is never ascertained by inspecting the organ. The hands may become " large and sinewy " in many ways besides in the business carried on where " the village smithy stands." While the destructive propensity may find honourable vent in the battlefield, and other legitimate quarters, it is not to be wondered at that we meet with many persons unhanged having heads no better in form than those of others who have been hanged.

Our actions are not at all times regulated by a previous consultation between the opposing faculties. The best of us are sometimes swayed by emotional feelings, and the dullest are often guided by reason. Phrenology explains these turns of character by representing the human mind as consisting of various distinct faculties, which may act singly or in unison ; also by claiming the brain as consisting of a multiplicity of different organs, some of which may be exercised during the repose of others.

We now come to the culminating point of Dr. Wilson's article where he says: " To proceed further would be to slay the slain."   Notwithstanding this he continues to hack the dead.

He objects to the cerebellum as being the organ of the function which the first cerebral physiologists traced to it.   He says: "We now know that the old Phrenology of the cerebellum is utterly wrong and unfounded.   The new Phrenology has shown us that in cases of diseased animal appetites—which in our lunatic asylums are but too frequently represented—the cerebellum is not found to be affected, a result explained by the fact that the appetites referred to are indeed as much a part of our 'mental' constitution as is the exercise of Benevolence or any other mental faculty."

When he says *diseased* animal appetites, he does not mean *diseased* but *morbid*.   His much-lauded new Phrenology proves the old Phrenology wrong, because an irrepressible desire is found where the cerebellum is un-affected.   Vigorous function in connection with sound organ. As to Amativeness being a mental faculty, the phrenologist must feel greatly indebted for the information ; very much so indeed.

As another discovery of the new Phrenology, Dr. Wilson quotes an account of the experiments made by M. Flourens many years ago, and now quite hacknied. He says: "Furthermore, the new Phrenology supplies positive evidence as to the true function of the cerebellum. When it is removed from a pigeon, for instance, the animal retains its faculties; it will feed, it can see and hear, but is utterly unable to maintain its equilibrium. But with its cerebellum present, and *minus* its true brain, the bird can perfectly co-ordinate its movements. It will fly straight if thrown into the air, it will walk circumspectly enough if pushed forwards, and will exhibit, in fact, such perfect muscular control, despite its want of volitation and intellect, that the functions of the cerebellum, as a controller of movements, are no longer matter of hypothesis, but become stable physiological fact."

While, by such results, the physiologist feels justified in regarding animal locomotion as dependent on the cerebellum, yet this being its physical function does not prove that the mental faculty traced to it by the phrenologists is not also a function of the cerebellum.

Instances are not wanting to show that these seemingly different functions are correlated, and thereby corroborate the fact that both appertain to the same organ. It is well known that a tendency to act with vehemence finds alleviation in the exercise of the mental function of the cerebellum ; while restraint or denial in this particular induces a restive state, sometimes resembling madness, unless where vented in epileptic fits. Stimulants partaken of immoderately affect the equilibrium and excite the propensity now alluded to at the same time.

As if it were a discovery of modern research, Dr. Wilson quotes the now old American crow-bar case, where a man, whilst engaged in blasting rocks, had a bar of iron forced through the left side of his skull, in at the front and out at the top; and who recovered from this accident and lived for twelve years after, without any apparent loss of his mental powers.

From this Dr. Wilson concludes: "That the organs of the phrenologist are mere theoretical nonentities, without a trace of substance to ensure their stability or real nature." This naturally comes from his not having learned anything about Phrenology, or he would have known that it first taught us that the opposing hemispheres of the brain perform the same functions, and that the side left intact did the business of the missing parts of the other side; just as persons continue to see with one eye after injury to the other.

D

The rest of Dr. Wilson's article is merely a repetition of what Professor Ferrier has already published, his transcription containing even the false inferences of that authority. For instance, Professor Ferrier says: "The sense of touch is not localised in the convolutions on the exterior surface of the brain, and this is rather a serious fact for the phrenologist, who localises all the faculties here. The sense of touch is localised in the internal, or inner surface, of the hemisphere."

Here the Professor assumes that the sense of touch is included among the phrenological organs which occupy the exterior surface of the brain; but this is contrary to the truth; while the fact that the organ or ganglion of the nerves of touch or feeling has its place in the inner surface of the hemisphere, and beyond the reach of the observer; and that it is omitted in the busts, goes a long way to vouch for the correctness of the others, seeing that the phrenologists have not represented on the outer surface of the brain this one organ, which is now ascertained to occupy a position in the innermost recess of the brain.

Dr. Wilson then repeats what Professor Ferrier says with regard to *asphasia*—a malady by which the patient is reduced to a state of speechlessness, although still capable of understanding what is said. The seat of the disease producing this effect is invariably found at the lower frontal lobe, which lies behind the orbit of the eye, to which part the phrenologists have traced the organ of language or memory of words. Such being the function of this part, the patient is able to remember words by the opposite side, which remains unaffected; although incapable of speech, because the tongue, though a duplex or bilateral member, is but a single body, and its movements are therefore dependent on healthful function in both sets of its guiding nerves, and fails to observe the dictates of one set ; just as a bird fails in the act of flying with one wing pinioned. In this manner Phrenology explains what Professor Ferrier, and everyone else unacquainted with Phrenology, is unable to account for. This explanation certainly holds out no hope for the asphasic patient, such as promised by Professor Ferrier, when he says: "It is quite conceivable that a person who has become asphasic by reason of total and permanent destruction of the left speech centre, may re-acquire the faculty of speech by education of the right articulatory centres."

The only chance for the patient is that the diseased part may right itself, which is quite possible upon phrenological principles, by which the brain is regarded as all of a piece with the rest of the body, and that it therefore partakes of its general qualities, one of which is that of renewing itself after disease.

Every case brought forward by the modern phisiologist clearly proves that the brain is a plurality of organs each having particular functions. How, with this fact before him, Dr. Wilson could possibly fall into the error of making such an assertion as "That there is no trace of a single organ such as the phrenologist theoretically maintains is represented in the brain," seems most strange, unless he had turned his attention inwardly. The fact of the matter is that what Dr. Wilson thought was Phrenology, was not Phrenology at all, but merely a phantom of his own creating, which he has most successfully vanquished, no doubt, to his satisfaction. Until the cerebral organs shall emerge right through the skull and proclaim their presence at every turn of the mind—like the bird which starts out from the toy clock and sings "cuckoo" with the chiming of every hour—until then, every sciolist emboldened by a sufficiency of scurrilousness, must assail Phrenology and chase it to the haunts of fortune-telling and other craft of witches.

On first beholding the brain, its intricate windings naturally bewilder the observer, and lead to the idea that any attempt to unfold its uses must be utterly futile. It is on this account that the brain, until the discovery of Phrenology, remained but as a dead letter in physiological science. The study of the mind

at first presents difficulties in no less a degree. Hence
the innumerable theories of the mind, each contra-
dictory of the other, and all fallacious in their explica-
tions of the mental system.

Phrenology, by embracing both departments of
study, mind and brain, has successfully solved two
problems, which singly had baffled all previous attempts
to explain satisfactorily. The undertaking naturally
presents itself as onerous if not absolutely impossible.
Hence it finds no favour in the scientific class-room,
where it is either pooh-poohed, or the attention is
too much engrossed with monkeys and fossils to
consider its claims.

To accept Phrenology upon faith is an easy matter,
but to understand it is to engage in a study of the most
abstruse kind, presenting, as it does, principles which,
at first sight seem self-conflicting and repugnant to
previously cherished views.

Thus beset, the vacillating novice may turn from the
task, as being likely to lead to nothing but a jumble of
contradictions, unless he is induced to engage in it with
the view of exposing its apparent fallacies; but it is
then that he is taken in his own snare, and himself
becomes converted. Many who have started upon the
study of Phrenology in this spirit have ultimately
become its ablest propounders and most zealous advo-

cates.   Mr. Abernethy was an instance, if we may judge from the following extracts.   When lecturing on the phrenological doctrines to the Court of Assistants of the College of Surgeons of London, in 1821, after discussing the nature of the faculties to the exercise of whose functions the different organs of the brain subserve, and the situations of these organs, Mr. Abernethy says:

"In looking over the list of faculties, in order to see if I could reconcile them to analogy and reason, I could discern no order nor connection between them.   The whole presented to me a rude appearance quite different, as I then thought, from what is found in Nature.   But after a more attentive consideration, light began to dawn upon me; and, beginning to consider the faculties in a certain way and to group them after a certain order, the whole gradually formed themselves before me into a system of surprising symmetry; and—like the disjointed parts of an anamorphosis, when seen from the proper point of view, collecting themselves under one elegant design—delighted me with the appearance of that very order and beauty that I would beforehand have expected to find in the mental faculties.   The *harmonious junction of the organs*, the beautiful adaptation of the faculties to each other, and to the phenomena of mind, as observable in every state in which it exists, are far too remarkable, and the coincidences far too numerous and exact, to have occurred by chance.

"As soon would a number of letters shaken out of Swift's laputian machine fall of themselves into a scientific treatise, as would the names of thirty-five or six faculties, put down at random, compose a complete and well-combined scheme of the human mind, such as this appears actually to be. The inference is, I think, irresistible, either that the scheme, which appears so well arranged, has been invented by Drs. Gall and Spurzheim, or (if they actually proceeded, as they tell us, and found it piecemeal by a gradual and patient examination of facts) that the harmony and systematic junction of these scattered members forms a very strong presumption—to say no more—in favour of the accuracy of their separate observations, and of the system being truly founded in Nature.

"Had Drs. Gall and Spurzheim sat down with the purpose of constructing a system from their own imagination, it is next to morally impossible that they could have contrived one which harmonises so completely with itself, and with the actual state of the mental faculties, and the uses to which these faculties are subservient. This is a problem which has puzzled the most eminent philosophers of ancient and modern times; and all attempts to solve it have hitherto been fruitless, so as almost to conclude that its solution was beyond the reach of human ingenuity.

" If, then, these gentlemen have actually succeeded in inventing a system like this, which affords a key to the mental constitution of man, and a facility of accounting for the diversities of human character and intellect, far surpassing any other system that has ever yet appeared—supposing it to be, as all other systems have been, purely hypothetical—it would entitle its authors to rank as philosophers with the highest names that ever have adorned the annals of the world."

Thus guided by so competent an authority, every medical man set up a phrenological bust in his surgery, in recognition of the respect which he entertained for the phrenological doctrines. This became so general that a surgery was considered to be but incompletely furnished without such a bust; and a phrenological head was a regular item in the order for an outfit such as supplied to medical men by the firm of Messrs. Maw, Son, and Thompson, surgical-instrument makers, of London. The example thus set by the surgeons was followed by the chemists, who, from the erudite appearance which it gave, placed a phrenological head in their windows. Thus exposed, these busts often found a sale among the general public. To keep up appearances with their betters, the quack doctors exhibited them in recommendation of their profession. This so disgusted the chemists that many of them discontinued to show them.

The phrenological heads were adopted by the opticians originally to show spectacles on, who, finding a sale for them, have continued to keep them ever since; and from a brief glance at one of these heads Dr. Wilson was induced to jump at such latitudinous conclusions about their presumptuousness.

As to the experiments made upon the living brain with electricity, which have been resumed for some years now, nothing through them has been elicited to lead to anything definite concerning the functions of the brain. Even the discovery of the speech centre is not due to such experiments, but to pathology; nor does there seem to be any prospect of their being of the least avail in this respect.

The manner in which such experiments are conducted renders success in this quarter altogether impossible. A monkey, or some other dumb animal, is by the application of chloroform reduced to a state of apparent insensibility, and thereby rendered incapable of manifesting any kind of emotion of a mental nature. After a part of the skull being cut away, electricity is applied to a particular part of the brain thus exposed,

and a particular limb of the animal is seen to contract
or move; a certain other part of the brain is irritated
and another limb is seen to be similarly affected; the
phenomena being of a purely physical character without
a single vestige of thought or feeling; just as seen in
the puppet, where "you pull the string and the figure
moves." By proving beyond doubt that particular parts
of the brain subserve to distinct and particular functions,
one, at least, of the phrenological propositions becomes
in part substantiated; beyond this, with one exception
to be named presently, these experiments are but tanta-
mount to killing the goose for the golden eggs. This
was observed many years ago by Mr. Lawrence, who
says: "Living bodies, as well as all dead ones, exhibit
electrical phenomena under certain circumstances; but
the contrast between the animal functions and electric
operations is so obvious and forcible, that the attempts
to assimilate them do not demand further notice."

So much then for the new Phrenology, as anticipated
to be the outcome of the experiments conducted by
Professor Ferrier, which Dr. Wilson has so much ex-
tolled, and which was to blast Phrenology, the only
physiology of the brain. As Mr. Lawrence remarks:
"If the mental processes be not the function of the
brain, what is its office? In animals, which possess only
a small part of the human cerebral structure, sensation

exists, and in many cases more acute than in man. What employment shall we find for all that man possesses over and above this portion—for the large and prodigiously developed human hemispheres? Are we to believe that these serve only to round off the figure of the organ, or to fill the cranium?"

Guarded by the stern rules of inductive reasoning, Phrenology stands fixed and pre-eminent among the sciences; while the ignoble sophistry raised against it falls unavailable as a shadow cast by the feeble.glimmer of a three-farthing rush-light against the rocks of Gibraltar, in the attempt thereby to overturn them.

That most of the sciences owe their perfection to the aid they receive one from the other as also to the arts, is a well-known fact. The astronomer has been greatly assisted by the optician, whose art has proved useful in navigation and many other departments. The physiologist has derived much information concerning the elementary nature of the fluids secreted by the different organs of the body, from the researches of the chemist, and by which the physician is enabled to judge what drugs are suitable for particular affections. Indeed, in this way the physiologist has been guided concerning the functions of the internal organs from their becoming excited to functional activity by the employment of such agents as affect them. But while physiologists have taken advantage of thus tracing function to organ, they have hitherto overlooked what may be the function of the grey matter of the brain by a similar mode of investigation.

Electricity being the only agent by which the brain and nervous system is incited to anything resembling functional activity, the inference seems just that the brain is an electrical apparatus.

The white matter has already been ascertained to be but as the conducting wires or messengers; the grey matter overlying that being all that is left of the brain; it is in this alone that we must suspect the function thus pointed to it by electricity.

The telegraphic wires would environ the wide world over and over in vain but for the cells or batteries which generate their vitality. A part corresponding to such cells or batteries is necessary to complete the telegraphic system of the animal body.

Besides serving as the coping-stone in the brain's architecture, the grey matter of the brain is to the nervous system what the heart is to the arterial system. It fulfils the duties of both chemist and purveyor to the nervous system in general. Being itself nourished by the arteries which ramify its surface, the grey matter generates an electrical fluid, giving vital force to the whole nervous system. The cerebellum serving as reservoir and safety-valve to the cerebrum, regulates the distribution of this fluid.

An insufficient supply of blood to the brain results in nervous depression, or want of mental energy and languor of body; while the opposite condition, restlessness and excitability even to a dangerous degree, arises from an excess of electricity in the nervous system due to a superfluity of blood to the brain.

The skull, by its divisions or sutures, is so arranged as to resist external pressure, but to yield and admit of expansion from internal pressure sufficiently to allow for the tidal flow of the blood without interrupting the brain's action.

A sudden eruption of blood to the head, by pressing upon the brain, checks the action of the grey matter, and induces prostration of body, accompanied by what is called a state of stupefaction, or a suspension of the mental powers. A patient in this condition is generally treated in a manner which tends less to accelerate recovery than to retard, if not to check it altogether. When what is now explained as the function of the brain becomes recognised, the following treatment will suggest itself in such cases :—

The patient, as hitherto, should not be left to lay horizontally, as this position allows of continued effusion of blood to, and therefore pressure upon, the brain, which but augments the malady. Any means by which a nearly perpendicular position can be maintained, as by a mould padded so as not to check circulation at any part of the body, is best. Ice, or anything cold, should not be applied to the top of the head, as this would congeal the blood and irremovably fix the cause of the affection. Cold wet cloths should be applied to the back, or nape, of the neck near the cerebellum, so as to check an upward flow of the blood in its circulation. Animation is continued by functional activity in the corporeal organs which, by continuity of action, will ultimately absorb the surplus blood of the body, and thereby relieve the brain, and so render recovery possible. A little bloodletting might be even beneficial.

A more expeditious treatment, which suggests itself in such cases, is to open the skull at one of the highest sutures, and remove the extraneous matter staying the brain's action.

Where recovery of the patient is dependent on such an operation being performed, the operator will not regard it as more dangerous than that of turning an eye by the occulist, or than amputating a limb by the surgeon; and where death is inevitable but by such means, there will be nothing to risk, while the probability of success makes the trial worth venturing.

It is well known to the medical faculty that large

portions of the brain may be cut away without causing the least pain to the patient, though he be perfectly conscious when this is being done.

But this subject must be treated in a subsequent issue, as to consider all its bearings here would be a digression in this reply to Dr. Andrew Wilson's attack on Phrenology.

While the brain is thus taken up—the white matter in conducting our movements, and the grey in giving vitality to the white—in our simplicity we might be inclined to suppose that if the brain be thus entirely utilised, with nothing of it left to represent the mind, Phrenology must forego its claim of the mind's connection with the brain. But this idea will fall through as we learn to distinguish between organ and function. It betokens a narrowness of judgment to seek the mind in the instrument through which it manifests itself.

Mind is related to the brain in the same manner as is the grandeur to the architecture of St. Paul's Cathedral, which is not the material, but a result of the disposition of the material. To appreciate the beauty of St. Paul's Cathedral it is necessary to view it at a distance, but if the observer be too short-sighted thus to survey its beauty, he will certainly fail to see it by an examination of its particles even if he were aided by the combined power of all the microscopes in the world.

It is in its *uses* that the brain claims connection with the mind, and not in itself. As well might we look for intelligence *in the ink* upon this paper. The arrangement of the ink may both display and convey intelligence, but the ink itself is not intelligence.

The brain is, as it were, the mind's ink-pot, which may contain what will serve to display every letter of the mind's volume; but it is not, therefore, the mind.

Be it ethereal or otherwise, the mind, as it manifests itself to our senses, is a phase or attribute of the brain's order. What the mind is, apart from the brain, is beyond the province of the phrenologist to tell.

THE END.

PRINTED BY CASSELL, PETTER, GALPIN & CO., LUDGATE HILL, LONDON, E.C.